I Can Read!

SHARED
My First
READING

Axel
THE TRUCK

Beach
Race

Story by **J. D. Riley**

Pictures by **Brandon Dorman**

Greenwillow Books, *An Imprint of* HarperCollins*Publishers*

Adobe Illustrator was used to prepare the full-color art.

www.icanread.com

Library of Congress Cataloging-in-Publication Data is available.
ISBN 978-0-06-222230-5 (hardback)— ISBN 978-0-06-222229-9 (pbk. ed.)

18 19 20 LSCC 10 9

Greenwillow Books

For the kids who love things that go
—J. D. R.

For my fast-as-lightning nephew AB!
—B. D.

Axel is a red truck.

Axel has big, big wheels.

"I like to go fast," Axel says.

"My engine is loud," Axel says.

Vroom, vroom, varoom!

Axel likes to have fun.

He likes to get dirty.

Axel says, "Look out, mud!"

Glup, glup, goop!

Axel rolls down the road.

He rolls past the town.

Axel's big tires zoom around.

His big tires spin fast.

Zip, zip, zoom.

Axel speeds to the beach.

Axel races the waves.

He races the fish.

15

Honk! Honk! Bronk!

Axel races the big trucks.

Axel wins!

Axel gets sand in his wheels.

He gets salt on his windows.

Crunch, crunch, crack.

"It is time for Thunder Wash!"
Axel says.

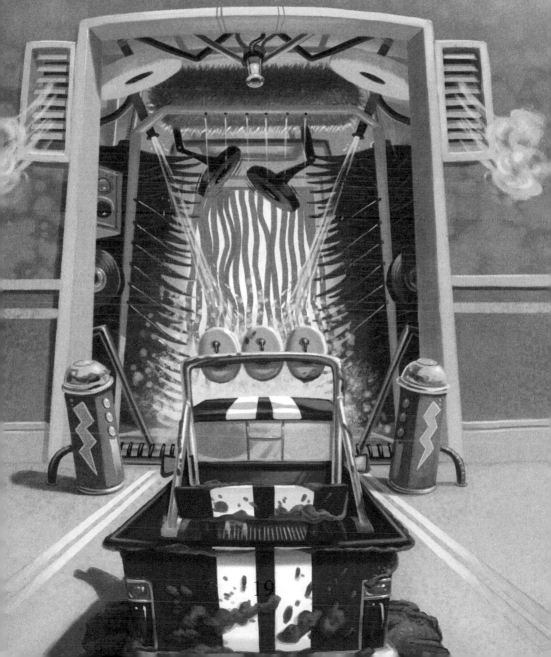

19

The water in the truck wash sprays up and down.

Water jets spray
around and around.
Bam, bam, slam!

The sand and salt are gone.

It's time to roll back home.

23

"Look out, mud!" Axel says.

"Here I come again!"

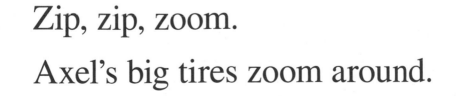

Zip, zip, zoom.

Axel's big tires zoom around.

Vroom, varoom!

Beep, beep!

That was monster fun.

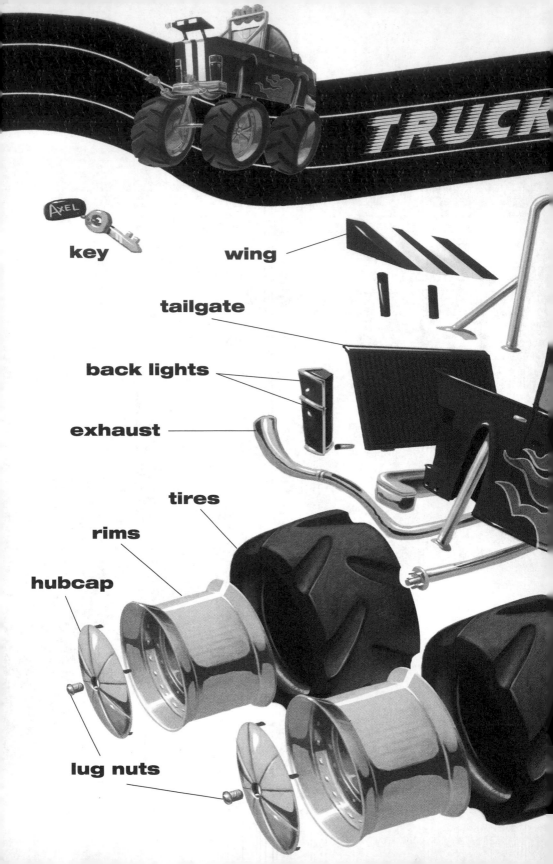

TRUCK

key

wing

tailgate

back lights

exhaust

tires

rims

hubcap

lug nuts

Dear Parent:
Your child's love of reading starts here!

Every child learns to read in a different way and at his or her own speed. Some go back and forth between reading levels and read favorite books again and again. Others read through each level in order. You can help your young reader improve and become more confident by encouraging his or her own interests and abilities. From books your child reads with you to the first books he or she reads alone, there are I Can Read Books for every stage of reading:

SHARED READING
Basic language, word repetition, and whimsical illustrations, ideal for sharing with your emergent reader

BEGINNING READING
Short sentences, familiar words, and simple concepts for children eager to read on their own

READING WITH HELP
Engaging stories, longer sentences, and language play for developing readers

READING ALONE
Complex plots, challenging vocabulary, and high-interest topics for the independent reader

ADVANCED READING
Short paragraphs, chapters, and exciting themes for the perfect bridge to chapter books

I Can Read Books have introduced children to the joy of reading since 1957. Featuring award-winning authors and illustrators and a fabulous cast of beloved characters, I Can Read Books set the standard for beginning readers.

A lifetime of discovery begins with the magical words **"I Can Read!"**

Visit www.icanread.com for information
on enriching your child's reading experience.